A FLIP-FLOP ADVENTURE!

Flip-Flop
and the
Absolutely Awful New Baby

By Janice Levy

Illustrated by
Colleen Madden

magic Wagon

visit us at www.abdopublishing.com

Published by Magic Wagon, a division of the ABDO Group, 8000 West 78th Street, Edina, Minnesota 55439. Copyright © 2012 by Abdo Consulting Group, Inc. International copyrights reserved in all countries. All rights reserved. No part of this book may be reproduced in any form without written permission from the publisher.

Looking Glass Library™ is a trademark and logo of Magic Wagon.

Printed in the United States of America, North Mankato, Minnesota.
052011
092011
 This book contains at least 10% recycled materials.

Written by Janice Levy
Illustrations by Colleen Madden
Edited by Stephanie Hedlund and Rochelle Baltzer
Cover and interior design by Jaime Martens

Library of Congress Cataloging-in-Publication Data

Levy, Janice.
  Flip-Flop and the absolutely awful new baby / by Janice Levy; illustrated by Colleen Madden.
      p. cm. – (A Flip-Flop adventure)
  Summary: At first Flip-Flop thinks the new baby is weird, but after Mom says she is staying, Flip-Flop takes another look at her sister.
  ISBN 978-1-61641-651-5
  [1. Frogs–Fiction. 2. Animals–Infancy–Fiction. 3. Sisters–Fiction.] I. Madden, Colleen M., ill. II. Title.
  PZ7.L5832Fld 2011
  [E]–dc22
                              2010048710

The new baby is **weird**.
Absolutely awful.

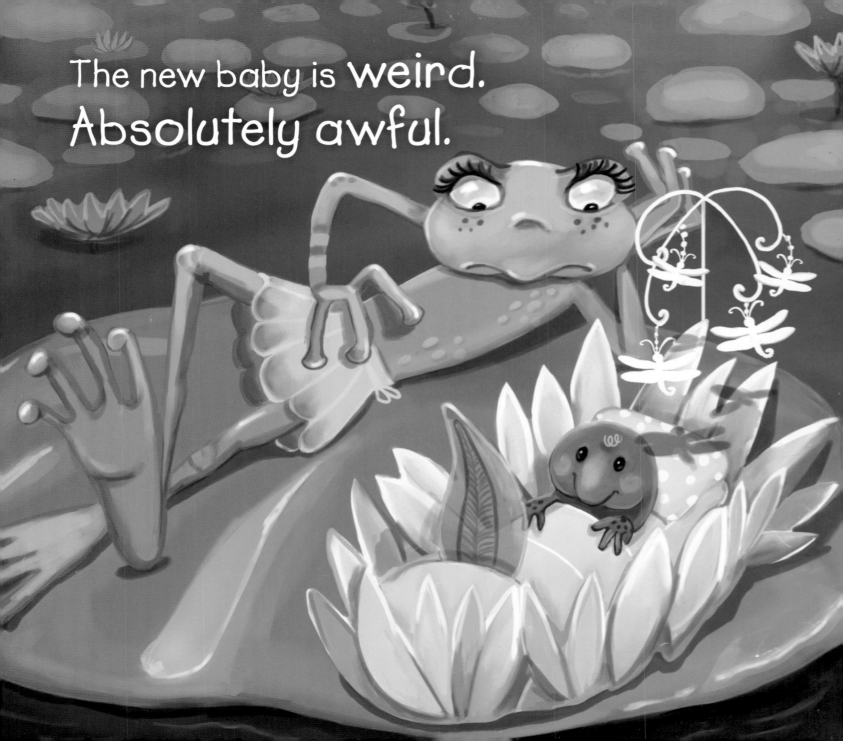

Bugs fly up her nose.

When she dives, she belly flops.

Everything she eats is **mushy**.

Mom calls her Cutie Patootie.
I call her Pop Eyes.

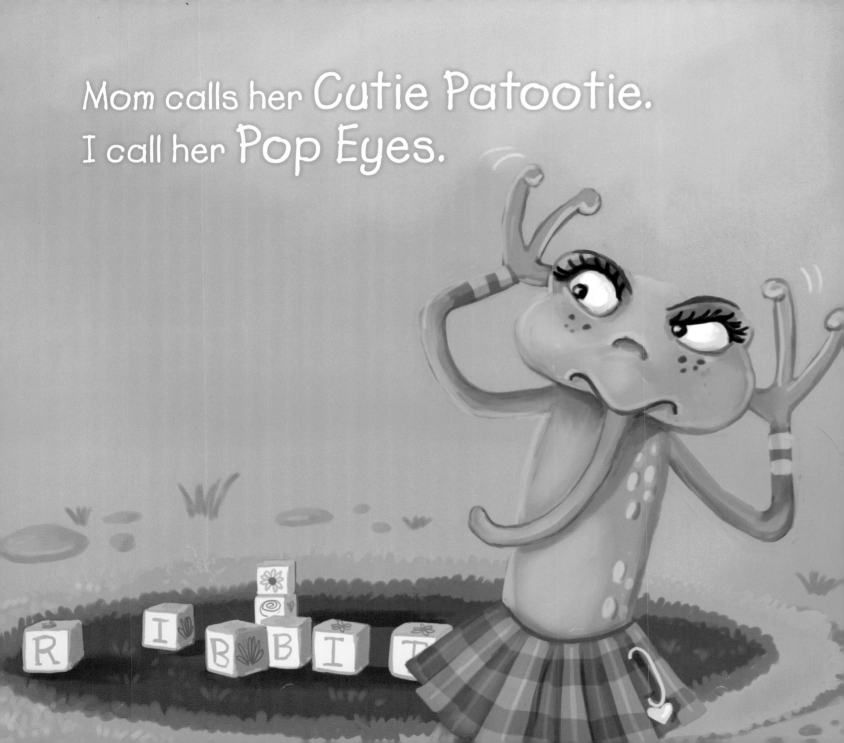

She's too tiny to play leapfrog.

Or jog in the park.

Mud wrestling?

Pop Eyes would never think of scuba diving.

Or surfing.

Camping out?
I don't **think** so.

Hopping makes her dizzy.

Worms gross her out.

She croaks like
a **cricket**.

crooohhrrk!
crooohhrrk!

Pop Eyes is weird.
Absolutely awful.
But Mom says she's staying.
So, I better take another look . . .

Pop Eyes doesn't call me Wart Nose.
Or splash water in my face.
She hates bullies, too.

She never interrupts me when I'm talking.
Doesn't care if I sing off-key.
She giggles at all my jokes.

Pop Eyes doesn't yell
when I forget to do stuff.
Or mess up magic tricks.
(Well, maybe just a little.)
We both think it's okay to cry.

She lets me check under rocks
for monsters.
And leave the night-light on.
She doesn't share my secrets.

Pop Eyes says I'm awesome.

Absolutely.

Her real name is Phoebe.
Maybe there's hope for her yet.

Flip-Flop FUN

At first, Flip-Flop didn't like the new baby!
Have you had a new baby brother or sister?
What did you think of him or her?

Once your brother or sister got older, you probably found lots of things to do together, just like Flip-Flop and Phoebe. What do you like to do with your siblings?

Think of one nice thing you can do for your little brother or sister. Do that nice thing to make him or her smile!

About the Author: Janice Levy is the author of numerous award-winning children's books. Topics include bullying, multiculturalism, foster care, intergenerational relationships, and family values. She teaches creative writing at Hofstra University. Her adult fiction is widely published in magazines and anthologies.

About the Illustrator: Colleen Madden is an illustrator, mom, kickboxer, ukulele strummer, and honorary frog. She loves to draw for kids (and kids at heart!) and make people giggle. Flip-Flop is her third series of children's books. She is currently writing her own titles as author/illustrator, which will all be very silly books.